NINA

BBC CHILDREN'S BOOKS
Published by the Penguin Group
Penguin Books Ltd, 80 Strand, London WC2R 0RL, England
Penguin Books Australia Ltd, 250 Camberwell Road,
Camberwell, Victoria 3124, Australia
First published by BBC Worldwide Ltd, 2000
Text and design © BBC Children's Books, 2000
This edition published by BBC Children's Books, 2005
CBeebies & logo™ BBC. © BBC 2002
10 9 8 7 6 5 4
Written by Diane Redmond
Based upon the television series
Bob the Builder © 2005 HIT Entertainment PLC and Keith Chapman.
The Bob the Builder name and character and the Wendy, Spud, Roley,
Muck, Pilchard, Dizzy, Lofty and Scoop characters are trademarks of
HIT Entertainment PLC. Registered in the UK.
With thanks to HOT Animation
www.bobthebuilder.com
All rights reserved.
ISBN 1 405 90071 7
Printed in Italy

Mucky Muck

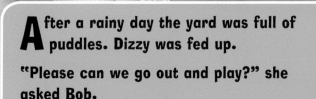

After a rainy day the yard was full of puddles. Dizzy was fed up.

"Please can we go out and play?" she asked Bob.

"No, Dizzy," he said. "You'll get dirty, just like Scoop and Muck."

"But it's lovely being dirty!" cried Muck.

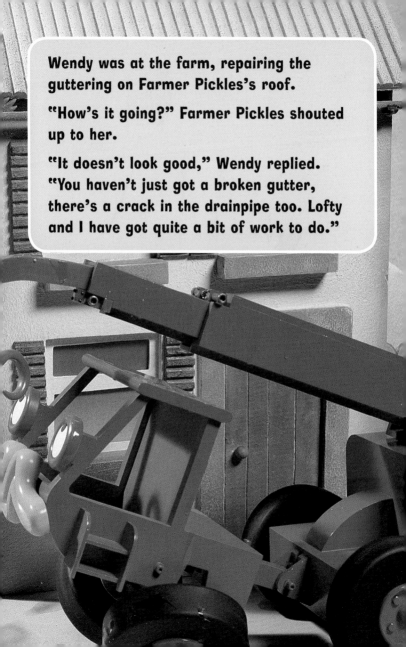

Wendy was at the farm, repairing the guttering on Farmer Pickles's roof.

"How's it going?" Farmer Pickles shouted up to her.

"It doesn't look good," Wendy replied. "You haven't just got a broken gutter, there's a crack in the drainpipe too. Lofty and I have got quite a bit of work to do."

Back at the yard, Bob put on his apron and filled up a bucket with warm, soapy water.

"Who's first for a wash?" he asked.

Muck huddled up close to Roley. "I don't want to be washed. I love being mucky."

"That's why you're called Muck!" chuckled Roley.

Meanwhile, Spud had been sheltering from the rain in Travis's trailer.

"Thanks, Travis," he said. "I hate getting wet."

"That's all right," said Travis and revved up his engine to move forward.

His wheels span around, but Travis didn't move.
He was stuck in the deep mud.

"I'll never get out!" he wailed.

"Hang on," said Spud. "I'll go and get Farmer
Pickles."

Back at the yard, Bob had just finished giving Scoop a wash down.

"Right, now it's your turn, Muck," said Bob.

"Can Roley go before me?" he begged.

"You're not frightened of a drop of water, are you?" laughed Bob.

"No, of course not," said Muck, very nervously.

Just then, Bob's mobile phone started ringing.

"That was Farmer Pickles. Travis is stuck in the mud," he said.

"I can pull him out!" cried Scoop.

"Your wheels might get stuck too," said Bob. "I think I'll use Muck. His caterpillar treads are built for this kind of job."

"That's lucky," Muck whispered to Roley. "Now I can stay mucky!"

"Can we help him?" Bob called out.

"Yes, we can!" the machines shouted back.

Bob, Muck and Dizzy set off for the farm. When they arrived at the field, they could see that Travis was well and truly stuck.

"Don't worry, Travis," called Bob. "We'll have you out in no time." Bob tied one end of a rope around Travis's axle and the other end to Muck's tow bar.

"Can you tow it, Muck?" he called.

"YES... hummpf!" spluttered Muck as he struggled to turn his big caterpillar wheels. "I... Ufff! CAN!"

When Travis was free from the mud, Farmer Pickles invited them back to the farmhouse. On their way, Spud popped up, holding a big, sloppy mud pie.

"Hey, Dizzy, over here!" he called.

Dizzy turned around and Spud threw the mud pie straight into her face. Splat!

"A mud pie fight!" yelled Muck.

In their excitement, Dizzy and Muck forgot all about keeping up with Travis and Bob.

When Bob arrived at the farmhouse he found Lofty and Wendy fitting the last section of guttering.

"How are you getting on?" he called up to her.

"Fine," Wendy replied. "So you managed to pull Travis out of the mud?"

"Yes. Muck did well, didn't you?" Bob said as he turned around to talk to Muck. But he wasn't there. "Where have Muck and Dizzy gone?" he gasped.

Muck was still having a wonderful time in the field.

"If I was as little as you, Dizzy, I'd roll over and wriggle in this lovely, squishy mud!" he said.

"Wheee!" squeaked Dizzy as she rolled happily in the mud.

Suddenly they heard Bob's voice. "Dizzy! Muck! What's going on?" he shouted.

"Er, we were just having a game of mud pies," muttered Muck.

"We were worried. You had all better get back to the farm, right now," said Bob. "Farmer Pickles has got a surprise for you."

Back at the farm, Bob lined up Muck, Dizzy and Spud, and told them to close their eyes.

"Ooh, I hope it's something really scrummy!" said Spud hungrily.

"Ready?" Bob asked, as Wendy and Farmer Pickles came out of the house with buckets of soapy water.

"Ready!" laughed Wendy.

Wendy dipped her brush into the water and started to wash the mud off Dizzy's mixer.

"Ooh, ooh, that tickles!" Dizzy giggled. Muck wanted to open his eyes when he heard Dizzy laugh.

"No peeping, Muck!" called Wendy.

But when it came to Muck's turn he got a nasty shock.

"Arghh!" he yelled as Wendy splashed water all over him.

"Now it's your turn, Spud," said Farmer Pickles.

"Oh, no!" cried Spud. He turned to run away, but skidded in a muddy puddle.

"Owww!" Spud cried, as he fell flat on his face and bent his nose.

"Has anyone got a new parsnip?"

THE END!